ELLA
the Elephant

Written and Illustrated by

KURT WIESE

Author of
Karoo the Kangaroo
and
Wallie the Walrus

PUBLISHED IN NEW YORK BY

COWARD-McCANN, Inc.

Printed in the U. S. A.

Ella the Elephant

ELLA THE ELEPHANT

I

Down the slopes of the hills in India came the Monsoon, the wind which brings the rain. It slashed the rushing brook and made its water whirl and foam. It brushed over the grass and the jungle. It threw sheets of water over the country. In their leaking mud houses all the farmers sat, shivering—but happy. The rain came just in time to make their crops grow.

Deep in the jungle of a valley the raindrops dripped from leaf to leaf. They ran along the twisted branches and the creepers. They washed the dust off the plants and soaked the ground.

And in the midst of the dripping jungle, like a big grey rock, stood Mother Elephant; and, looking out into the rainy world as if from under an arch, stood Ella, her baby.

II

When Ella was born she was covered with black hair and her trunk was almost rosy. After two weeks she began to look different. Most of her hair was gone and her trunk became darker.

She was the happiest baby in the world. She played all day long, running quickly around her mother and through the four columns of her mother's legs. Her mother watched her every moment, holding her big trunk over the baby to protect her. When she didn't see her she called her in trumpeting tones and little Ella would answer with funny "peeps." Ella drank her mother's milk three times a day. At night Mother Elephant watched her sleep, swinging her big trunk over her and covering her with dry grass.

When Ella was two months old they both joined the herd, Ella walking under her mother. With the end of the rainy season the herd left the jungle and moved to the open plains where the grass was fresh and green. For the first time Ella ate grass. But she was still a baby, and so she drank some of her mother's milk as well.

III

At noon when the sun was hottest the herd rested in the shade of trees which stood in clusters, dotting the grassy plains. Some of the elephants picked a branch and beat their flanks with it; others took up dry sand with their trunks and threw it over their backs. They did this to keep the insects away. The leader moved his trunk all the time and sniffed the air watchfully.

In the afternoon the whole herd went down to the river to bathe. They rushed into the water and, filling their trunks, sprayed their dusty bodies. Some lay down and let the water cover them all up—except the tips of their trunks which they kept above the water in order to breathe. As Ella was not allowed to go into deep water, she had a shower bath out of her mother's trunk.

In the evening the herd went grazing again and during the night they slept. Most of the elephants lay down to sleep, but Ella's mother remained standing, swinging her trunk slowly over her baby who slept between her feet.

IV

One day the leader did not stop at the usual hour of rest. A strange feeling urged him to keep on marching. The baby elephant began to feel very tired. "Why do we have to travel so fast?" she asked her mother. Mother Elephant stopped for a moment to show Ella how to use her big ears. Ella flapped them slowly, and soon she heard the singing of the wind in the trees, and the trickling of the water over stones and leaves. She heard the hoarse voices of a flock of crows, and then—she heard another noise! It sounded as if a piece of loose bark slapped against a tree. And while Ella listened to this sound, her mother said:

"Look quickly! Do you see the little trees below the flying crows? Now watch—they are moving! Behind each tree a man is hidden. He will try to drive us towards other men. That is why we must move on very fast, without resting."

And with frightened eyes they joined the herd.

V

During that night there was not much rest for the elephants. Every now and then sudden little fires flared up in a wide half circle behind the herd and seemed to come nearer each time.

The next morning they heard the clatter of wood, which they did not know was made by rattles that the huntsmen used to confuse them.

When night came again, the fires had increased. They encircled the herd on all sides. The path left to the animals became very narrow. Suddenly shots were fired! Men shouted! Wood rattled! The elephants squeezed together and clouds of dust whirled up. Ella could not see her mother's legs any more. Then the noise and the fires were upon them.

In all this confusion, the elephants could still see an opening ahead of them. The leader crashed towards it and the herd followed. Trees fell across their path and, too late, they saw that they had run into an enclosure. A high fence made of whole tree trunks surrounded them, and on top of the fence sat dark men with blazing torches.

VI

Ella's mother looked for her baby. Her trunk groped through the excited crowd till at last she came to the fence. That stopped her search for a time. Then she thought only of the little elephant and did not mind the yelling men on top of the fence. She drew back for a moment, pressing those behind her till she got some room. She rolled up her trunk and then thrust herself against the wooden bars. Under her mighty weight the bindings of the railing snapped and the railing itself broke.

Just at this moment little Ella found her mother. When the logs crashed down, the baby elephant stood beside her. The next moment she went through the opening in the fence. But her mother never followed her. Strong ropes were slipped around her hind feet and she was tied to a big tree before she had noticed that the fence was down. Little Ella did not once look back—she thought her mother was following her and so she made straight for the dark and quiet of the jungle. When at last she stopped she found herself alone—too tired to think of anything but sleep.

VII

Through the opening in the leafy green roof over Ella's sleeping place a fine grey light hovered. It soon turned rosy and then trickled like gold from leaf to leaf. The sun was up. A wild peacock sat right above Ella and shouted, "Peeow, peeow!" which means "Good-morning."

Ella scrambled to her feet and stood a little dazed. Then she squeaked back, "Good-morning."

The bird came down a few branches and said in his rusty voice:

"Little elephant, listen to me. You are not safe here. This is the tiger's hunting ground and he has not eaten since last night. You must go away."

"Where shall I go? Where can I go?" cried Ella.

"Towards the sun, towards the sun," answered the peacock. "The tiger always runs away from the sun."

So Ella started off towards the sun.

VIII

The sun rose higher and higher.

When the hour of rest came, Ella walked more slowly till she reached a big rock covered all over with moss and creepers. Little streams of water ran down and formed a clear pool at the foot of the rock. Ella took a few trunkfuls of water and then leaned against the cool wall of the rock and fell asleep standing.

She awoke in the afternoon when the shadows had grown long. Something moved above her. She looked up over the edge of the rocks into many eyes staring at her. They belonged to the monkeys who had been there for a long time but who had kept quiet so that she might sleep undisturbed. Now they greeted her with loud chatters. And after they had heard her story, they said:

"Little elephant, it is late and the tiger will come out soon. You had better hurry and cross the river before he finds you."

Ella took another drink and hurried off towards the river.

IX

It was not long until the jungle opened and there lay the broad plain dotted with its groves of trees. Through it the river wound like a golden ribbon. Ella tramped the well-known paths through the grass and reeds that rimmed the river. When she came to the mud bank where the elephants used to bathe, she saw a piece of wood that she had never seen before. Ella stopped and strained her eyes. She flapped her ears and tried to catch a sound. Then her little trunk started winding and sniffing.

Did not a tiny eye gleam on the piece of wood? Yes! And there was a mouth wide open with long rows of sharp teeth. And along the mouth walked little birds who picked the remainder of the meal between those teeth. Yes! The thing which looked like a piece of wood was a crocodile. The crocodiles never dared to come near a herd of elephants, but they were not afraid of baby elephants, alone and unprotected.

Ella shivered and turned back to the reeds that closed behind her.

X

The reeds swayed in the evening breeze. Ella walked on, and soon they opened and a dark swamp lay before her. In the middle of the swamp stood a buffalo with his head raised and his horns curved wide against the evening sky.

The buffalo snorted:

"Little elephant, where are you going all alone?"

"I lost my mother when men trapped the herd," said Ella, "and now I'm trying to escape the tiger and get back to her, but I cannot cross the river because the crocodile is there."

The buffalo said:

"Stay with me during the night, little elephant. The tiger will not hurt you when I am around. In the morning, watch the parrots and follow them as they go down to the fields of men to feed. They are the men who caught your mother."

So Ella stayed with the buffalo. He was not at all afraid of the tiger. He had shaken him off his back and chased him away with his horns many times.

XI

The moon came up over the reeds like a big yellow wheel. She rose higher and higher and the sky grew dark. Then she stood like a silver disk on black velvet. She threw her silver into the river which braided a waving band of it across its dark back. The moon cast her soft light over the swaying reeds and over the back and the mighty horns of the buffalo who grazed quietly around the sleeping baby elephant. The silver moonbeams fell also on the striped body of the hungry tiger who circled around the buffalo's grazing ground, not daring to growl.

When he saw the buffalo standing on guard, ever watching and scenting, the tiger trotted back to the hills. He was very hungry, and he would have liked nothing better than a baby elephant for his meal. Instead he had to catch a wild pig, and when he had eaten until he could not swallow another mouthful, he crawled into his cave just before the sun rose.

XII

When Ella opened her eyes after a long, refreshing sleep, she saw the kind buffalo lying beside her. He had kept her warm during the chilly hours of the night. She thanked him by pressing her little trunk around his neck and then she got up to watch for the parrots.

The brightly colored birds were already down at the river, taking their morning drink. Just when the first rays of the sun trembled over the reeds, they came back in a large flock. Their feathers gleamed and sparkled with all the colors of the rainbow, and Ella could easily see the way they were going. Along the river, the glittering, shrieking birds flew, and after some time they turned inland.

When Ella reached the spot where she had seen the parrots last, a new and strange sight met her.

XIII

From the top of the hill on which she stood, the little elephant could look down into a valley divided into many fields of green and yellow. Behind the fields stood groups of dark trees and somewhere smoke curled up. Ella suddenly remembered the night of the capture. Her heart skipped a beat. She heard the parrots screeching and encouraging her and she went down, step by step, till she stood at the edge of a yellow cornfield.

The birds were everywhere, climbing up and down the corn stalks to get at the cobs which they broke with their strong beaks. All at once, the whole flock whirled up into the air, shrieking and flying rapidly back over Ella towards the woods.

Ella stood and watched. Her trunk quivered and her ears flapped in search of the reason for the birds' sudden departure. She started to turn back also, but a rope flew through the air and fell around her neck. She shrank back, afraid to look at the men who had rushed out of the field. Another rope lashed her hind leg, and the baby elephant was a prisoner again.

XIV

The dark men dragged and pushed the little elephant along the field towards the trees and the smoke. It seemed to Ella as if mingled with the smell of the smoke there was some other smell that made her heart glow. From time to time it seemed to her that the wind brought her a breath of her mother.

The road widened into the shade of the trees. Ella held her trunk lifted, sniffing eagerly. Her little eyes opened wide, her ears spread and with all her senses she felt the presence of her mother. She gave up trying to get away and rushed forward. There, under the biggest tree, stood her mother, trumpeting and struggling to get to her baby. She was still tied, but in her eyes there was no more terror of men—only happiness at seeing her baby again.

The ropes which bound Ella were loosened and the next moment the little elephant rushed up to her mother, and the small trunk and the large trunk wound around each other in sheer joy.

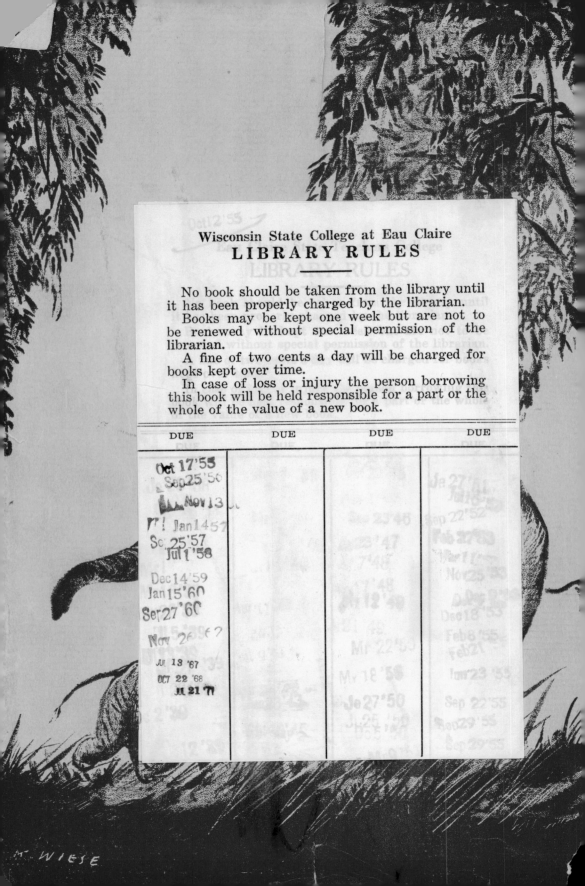

Wisconsin State College at Eau Claire
LIBRARY RULES

No book should be taken from the library until it has been properly charged by the librarian.

Books may be kept one week but are not to be renewed without special permission of the librarian.

A fine of two cents a day will be charged for books kept over time.

In case of loss or injury the person borrowing this book will be held responsible for a part or the whole of the value of a new book.

DUE	DUE	DUE	DUE
Oct 17'55			Ja 27'41
Sep 25'56			Jul 18
Nov 13		Ja 25'46	Sep 22'52
Jan 14'57		Ap 23'47	Feb 27'53
Se 25'57		J 7'48	Mar 1
Jul 1'58			Nov 25'53
Dec 14'59		Ap 7'48	Dec 9
Jan 15'60		Ju 12'49	Dec 18'53
Sep 27'60		Jy 49	Feb 8'55
Nov 26'62		Mr 22'55	Feb 21
JUL 13 '67		Mr 18'55	Nov 23'55
OCT 22 '68		Je 27'50	Sep 22'55
JUL 21 '71			Nov 29'55
			Sep 29'55

M. WIESE